CHRISTMAS BEAR

WRITTEN AND ILLUSTRATED BY SAL MURDOCCA

SIMON AND SCHUSTER BOOKS FOR YOUNG READERS
PUBLISHED BY SIMON & SCHUSTER INC.
NEW YORK

To my Mother, Rose

SIMON AND SCHUSTER BOOKS FOR YOUNG READERS, Simon & Schuster Building, Rockefeller Center,
1230 Avenue of the Americas, New York, New York 10020. Copyright © 1987 by Sal Murdocca. All rights
reserved including the right of reproduction in whole or in part in any form. Published by the Simon & Schuster
Juvenile Division. SIMON AND SCHUSTER BOOKS FOR YOUNG READERS is a trademark of Simon & Schuster
Inc. Designed by Malle N. Whitaker. Manufactured in the United States of America.
10 9 8 7 6 5 4 3 2   ISBN 0-671-64565-X

The last leaves were falling. The old bear's fur coat was now very thick. He knew that winter was coming. It always did.

"I'm getting sleepy," said Bear.

"You always do," said Robin.

"Will you wake me up in the spring?" asked Bear.

"I always do," replied Robin, "after I catch my first worm."

Bear made up his bed. He made a nice cup of hot chocolate and thought about the coming spring. He thought about the fresh fat trout in the melting streams. He thought about when he was young and was able to catch quick fishes. He thought about how he used to climb the trees and find the sweet new honey in old places. Then he put out the fire and closed his eyes.

Winter came. The cold winds from the north brought snow and ice. Bear's house grew cold. Bear was warm inside his fur coat under his warm quilted blanket. But Bear was old, and he could not sleep so easily anymore.

Bear looked out his window. He saw the fox chasing the rabbit. He saw Beaver's dam covered with quiet snow. He felt a slight chill and growled when he saw the far-off smoke from man's fire. He saw Raccoon walking by.

"Hello, Raccoon," said Bear.

"Hello, old-timer," said Raccoon. "Why aren't you in bed?"

"I'm thinking about the spring," said Bear.

"The sooner you sleep, the sooner it will be spring," said Raccoon.

"Have a nice winter," said Bear.

"Have a good sleep," said Raccoon, starting off.

"Be careful of the man's traps," said Bear. Then he went back to bed.

Finally Bear went to sleep. For weeks he dreamed of when he was a small cub and first tasted the fat fish and golden honey.

Then one day something went *Tap, tap, tap* at Bear's window.

"Go away!" growled Bear. "I'm in my sleep."

"Wake up!" said a tiny chirp. "It's me."

Bear growled softly and opened his window. There was Robin. It was nighttime, but the moon was full. He could see that the snow still covered the earth.

"It is not spring," said Bear.

"Help!" said Robin. "I have found a man in the snow."

"I do not like man," said Bear. But he left his house and followed Robin because he loved him.

Bear walked slowly through the snow. *Squeak, squeak*, went his big feet and paws. When they reached the part of the forest where the tall pines grew, Bear saw a small figure lying in the snow.

Bear came closer and saw that he was dressed in red.

He stood up on his hind legs and growled. But the little man lay still. Bear approached him and sniffed his face. It was not a bad smell.

Bear picked up the little man and carried him back to the house.

He put him to bed and waited for him to wake up.

Bear had trouble staying awake. He wanted to sleep again. He wanted to go back to his dreams about being young in the spring.

Bear began to fall asleep. Just as he had found a nice fat fish to dream about, the little man woke up.

"Where am I?"

"You are in my house," said Bear.

"Who are you?" said the man.

"I am a bear."

"I can see that," said the man. "I meant, what is your name?"

"Bear," said Bear thoughtfully. "Brown Bear."

The little man smiled. "Thank you, Bear," he said, "for saving my life."

"Who are you?" asked Bear.

"I am Santa Claus."

"Are you a hunter?" asked Bear. "Hunters wear red."

"I deliver presents," said Santa.

"Are you a postman?"

"No," said Santa, laughing. "Don't you know that tomorrow is Christmas?"

"I always sleep this time of year," said Bear.

"Well, I usually work this time of year," said Santa. "I deliver presents to children all over the world on this one night."

"What happened to you?" asked Bear.

"I was thrown from my sleigh when it hit one of those tall pine trees."

"Are you going back to work now?" asked Bear.

"I can't. I have hurt my hand and my leg. I don't think I can deliver all those presents. I'm afraid I'll have to ask for your help. There's no one else."

"But I'm supposed to be sleeping," said Bear.

"Do you want to disappoint all those children who expect to find presents in the morning?" said Santa.

Bear felt old and tired. He remembered that he had never been hunted by a child. "I suppose I can help you for one night."

"Good!" said Santa. "Now we must find my sleigh. It should be near where I fell out."

Bear growled and opened his door. "I'll be back as soon as I can."

Bear went back to where the tall pines grew. It was a big forest, and he did not know where to start. His sense of smell was not what it used to be. Then he heard the wolves.

When he found the sleigh, he also found eight tiny reindeer, all tangled up in their harnesses and reins. Surrounding them was Wolf and his pack of thirty.

"Go away, old bear!" said Wolf. "These are not fishes. This is the winter game. They belong to us."

The hair on Bear's back rose, and he stood up. He showed his broken teeth and roared so loudly that the icicles shook from the trees.

The wolves ran off. Before he disappeared, Wolf said, "This is not right. You should be sleeping."

"I know," said Bear.

"You are old and foolish," said Wolf.

"I know," said Bear.

Bear turned to the reindeer, who were afraid. "Don't worry," he said. "I was sent here by your Santa."

When Bear returned with the reindeer, he wrapped Santa in the warm quilted blanket and carried him outside. The reindeer were so happy to see him that they began to cry.

"Come, come, my darlings," said Santa. "There is much to do, and we have lost a lot of time."

In a few minutes Bear was ready to leave. He was wearing a red nightshirt and Santa's hat.

"How do I look?" asked Bear.

"The hat is a little small, but it will have to do," replied Santa.

"By the way," said Bear. "I do not know how to drive a sleigh. It is a human thing."

"Don't worry," said Santa, smiling. "My darlings have made this trip a thousand times. All you have to do is climb down the chimneys and put the presents under the trees or in the stockings."

Bear climbed into the sleigh. By now there were a few other animals who had come by to see what was going on. Bear waved good-bye to Robin, Santa, and the others.

Santa gave a short whistle, and the sleigh shot out and over the frozen lake before Bear knew what had happened.

"Oh, my goodness!" said Bear, looking down at the snow-covered earth.

It was a long night for Bear. He worked very hard in order to make up for all the lost time. He quickly learned how to use the reins and how to land on a roof. His only problem was sliding his big body down all those tight chimneys.

It was a long night for Santa and Robin. They could not sleep. When they saw the sun start to rise in the east, Santa hoped with all his heart that Bear had finished the work on time.

"Don't worry," said Robin. "Bear is very reliable. He goes to sleep and wakes up every year on the same two days."

Suddenly Santa pointed. "Look!" he said. "It's Bear!"

There in the morning sky, just ahead of the sun, was the sleigh, with eight tiny reindeer, sliding down on a ribbon of morning mist.

When Bear and the sleigh came to a stop, all the animals gave forth a great cheer of barks, chirps, whistles, and howls.

To a human it would have been the most frightening sound in the world. But to Bear it was the sound of his proudest moment.

When the small celebration was over, Santa made some hot chocolate. As they sipped from their mugs Santa asked, "How old are you, Bear?"

"Many springs," replied Bear. "I have known five robins."

"And what would you like more than anything in the world?"

Bear thought hard. Then he said, "I would like to be able to catch fish easily. I would love to be able to climb trees and find the honey again."

"I can't make you young," said Santa. "But I'll see what I can do."

When they finished their hot chocolate, Bear carried Santa
outside and put him into the sleigh.

"Thank you for everything," said Santa.

"You're welcome," said Bear. "It was a good thing to do."

"Have a merry Christmas!" said Santa as he snapped the reins
and gave a short whistle. "Let's go, my darlings!"

"Merry Christmas," said Bear as the sleigh shot out over the
mist on the lake.

Bear yawned loudly.

"You had better go to sleep," said Robin. "I'll wake you up in the spring."

"You always do," said Bear, entering his house.

Bear climbed into bed and closed his eyes. He tried to think about human children and whether they would like the taste of fresh fish and honey.

But after a while he began to dream his favorite dreams.

On the first day of spring Robin found a nice fat worm just
below the soil. He flew over to Bear's house and saw two
strange objects outside Bear's door.

Bear heard something go *Tap, tap, tap!* on his window.

"Is it spring already?" growled Bear.

"Hurry!" chirped Robin. "Two strange things are out here."

Bear grumbled softly and slowly opened his door.

"Thank you, Robin," he said.

"Look! Look there!" said Robin.

Bear looked at the two objects. One was a ladder and one
was a fishing net. A note read:

> Dear Bear,
> Have a merry spring!
> Love,
> Santa

That spring Bear caught the fat new fish and found the
golden honey in hiding places high up in the trees, and he felt
young again.